Christopher Anstey

The Patriot

A Pindaric address to Lord Buckhorse

Christopher Anstey

The Patriot
A Pindaric address to Lord Buckhorse

ISBN/EAN: 9783337308360

Printed in Europe, USA, Canada, Australia, Japan

Cover: Foto ©Andreas Hilbeck / pixelio.de

More available books at **www.hansebooks.com**

THE

PATRIOT,

A

PINDARIC ADDRESS

TO

LORD *BUCKHORSE.*

O ! mihi tam longæ maneat pars ultima vitæ,
Spiritus, et quantum fat erit tua dicere faƈta !

VIRG.

CAMBRIDGE,

Printed by FLETCHER and HODSON:

And fold by J. DODSLEY, in Pall-Mall ; S CROWDER, in Pater-Noſter-Row ;
J. ALMON, in Piccadilly ; and M. HINGESTON, near Temple-Bar, London.

MDCCLXVII.

TO

Lord BUCKHORSE,

IN VENERATION

OF HIS LORDSHIP's

PATRIOTIC VIRTUES,

THE FOLLOWING POEM

IS MOST HUMBLY INSCRIBED,

BY HIS LORDSHIP's

MOST DEVOTED,

MOST OBLIGED,

AND MOST OBEDIENT HUMBLE SERVANT,

Cambridge,
1767.   THE AUTHOR.

To Lord *BUCKHORSE.*

*WHILE you, my Lord, great *Drury*'s Weal fuftain,
Light ev'ry Walk, and open all the Lane,
With Strength of Arm plead *Black-boy Alley*'s Caufe,
Adorn with Manners, and improve with Laws;
Much would the Public fuffer from the Song
That dar'd, O BUCKHORSE, to detain thee long.

When *Alba*'s warlike Sons of Yore,
Held fage Debate on *Tyber*'s Shore,

* Vide HOR. Epift. 1. Lib. 2. *Cum tot fuftineas, &c.* .

B   A

A patriot Captain of Banditti

Was made their Chairman of Committee,

And plann d great *Rome*'s imperial City :

Where now, infhrin'd among the Gods,

With Joy he views, from Heav'n's Abodes,

Meek Cardinals, and holy Fryars,

For Learning fam'd; and chafte Defires,

Seafon the tender Minds of Youth

With Virtue, Liberty, and Truth :

Like him confign'd to glorious Reft

Amid the Regions of the Bleft,

No lefs, in thefe degen'rate Days,

A pious Knight demands our Praife,

Who, from an ardent Love of Knowledge,

Bequeath'd his Wealth to found a College.

And much we wifh, my Lord, that you.

Such bright Examples would purfue,

Build

Build here fome noble rich Foundation,

And form a Plan of Education

To mend the Morals of the Nation ;

Vifit yourfelf your own Afylum,

Statutes and wholfome Laws, compile 'em,

Nor fuffer Bifhops to embroil 'em ;

Correct their Manners, not fo gently

As Fame reports of Doctor B-NTL-Y,

But at th' Election of their Stewards,

Accept, my Lord, my Thoughts in few Words:

If fome important dull Logician,

Smit by the Dæmon of Ambition,

In pedant Politics officious

For *Machiavel* quits *Burgerfdicius* ;

Or like the great Men's Nomenclator ·

Tom Turbulent, that meddling Prater,

With

With Pertnefs, Pride, and Meannefs join'd

To vacant Head, and reftlefs Mind,

O'er thefe calm Realms, whence Science fprings,

Bids Difcord wave her baleful Wings,

Thefe bleft Abodes in Ferment puts——

—— Give him a Driver in the Guts,

And make fuch factious, ill-bred Chuckles,

Revere the Influence of your Knuckles;

Thus all their Feuds and Tumults quell,

And Peace reftore to *Ifrael* :

So may the Swans of *Camus* raife

Their tuneful Throats to chaunt thy Praife,

* *Granta* her Lift of Worthies crowning

With Names of BUCKHORSE and of DOWNING.

* Vide Commem. Benefact.

BACCHUS

* BACCHUS, when *India* was o'ercome,

And War compos'd by Wine and Rum,

(Which, you'll confefs yourfelf, my Lord,

Is better far than Fire and Sword)

To *Egypt* went, as rich as thofe

Who've feiz'd a Nabob by the Nofe;

And there, as ancient Bards relate,

Purchas'd a ruin'd 'Squire's Eftate;

Rubb'd up the Family Château,

Whofe Front three Window-Lights could fhew—

—The reft were dark'ned long ago:

There foon, by Jollity and Bounty,

Gain'd Int'reft both in Town and County;

* Vid. Dionyf. de fitu Orbis, lin. 1155.

C　　　　　　　　　　Cur'd

Cur'd an old May'r of drinking Water,

Sung Catches with his Wife and Daughter,

Sent Ven'son, which was kindly taken,

* And Woodcocks, which they boil'd with Bacon;

Created honorary Freemen,

Gave Toasts, and swallow'd more than three Men,

Granted, from fatherly Affection,

To ev'ry Voter his Protection,

Got drunk, and carry'd his Election;

A Work, my Lord, which all the World, next Year,

Expect from you, and many a Patriot Peer.

POLLUX, my Lord, and CASTOR too,

Were Bruisers both renown'd like you,

---

* *Quæq; ipse miserrima vidi.*   Virg.

Were

Were known at Cockpits, Fairs, and Races,

And bore their Links at public Places;

Now turn'd to heav'nly Conftellations,

Purfue their ancient Occupations :

Yet all thefe Heroes grew dejected,

When Favours they in Life expected,

Due to their Merits, were neglected.

For as our Eyes from far furvey,

Well-pleas'd, the glorious Lamp of Day,

Whofe near approaching Lines of Light

O'erpow'r and wound our aching Sight;

So Virtue, which offends when near,

Plac'd at a Diftance we revere,

And Patriots never, 'till remov'd,.

Or quite extinct, are prais'd and lov'd.

E'en

E'en He who cover'd with the Hide is

Of Lion flain, the great ALCIDES,

Who crufh'd the Hydra, and, what's more,

Subdu'd a Dragon and a *Boar*,

(Worfe than the Beaft who ravag'd long

The peaceful Vales of *Gevaudan*)

Who clear'd the Mews of King AUGEAS,

Stupendous Work ! and made fo free as

* To kick fuch Jockeys from his Stable,

As now, by gambling Tricks, are able

To treat whole Boroughs at their Table ;

Who, when a Child in Cradle laid,

On Necks of Snakes his Strength difplay'd,

---

* Vid. Paufan. in Eliacis, Plin. Lucian, &.

‡ Roaſt Beef, inſtead of Pap, would cram,

* Like Giant Boy of *Willingham* ;

From which ſuch Vigour was created,

† He *cuff'd* the Maid that on him waited,

And after that, to prove his Might,

Got fifty Children in a Night :

E'en He, for all his virtuous Labours,

Was damn'd and hated by his Neighbours,

And ev'ry Monſter overthrown,

Found Envy tam'd by Death alone.

On Thee, while yet alive, great Sir,

Maturer Honours we confer :

‡ Vid. Theocrit. Idyll. 23.
* Vid. Philoſ. Tranſact.
† Εx δ' ἀρ' ἄτλατον Βίλ℗
πλᾶξε Γυναῖκας,——*intolerabile vero jaculum percuſſit Mulieres.*
Pind. Od. Nem. 1. lin. 71. Oxon. Edit.

My

(**14**)

* My Mufe is ready to make Oath,

And fwear by Gods and Altars both,

We ne'er have feen, or e'er fhall fee,

A Patriot fo renown'd as thee.——

Oh! on the Swan's broad Pennons could I foar,

As erft the *Latian* Bard, new Tracts explore

O'er *Afric*'s Plains, o'er *Hyperborean* Shore

And *Afia*'s wide Domain! Ye facred Nine,

Daughters of JOVE, forfake the Throne divine,

Bear me, O bear me on your airy Wings

To *Twit'nam*'s laurel Groves, and filver Springs,

Where erft the Sage, 'mid *Thames*'s lift'ning Swains,

Attun'd th' *Horatian* Lyre to *Britifh* Strains;

* Ἀυδάσομαι ἰνόρκιον
λόγον.   Pind. Olymp. 2. l. 166.

Give

Give me, like him, to found my Patron's Praise,

And pluck one Garland of unfading Bays,

So to the World great BUCKHORSE I'll proclaim,

Enroll with Heroes and with Kings his Name,

And twine the Wreath immortal as his Fame.

I'll sing, my Lord, thy Trophies won.

On bloody Plains of *Kennington* ;

Sing how thy early Worth was prov'd,

'Mid Scenes of Death thy Soul·unmov'd,

What Time the Hangman's murd'rous Crew

The Rebels' mangled Entrails drew ;

Confusion reign'd, and dire Dismay——

Struck with Remorse, the God of Day

Turn'd his affrighted Beams away.

But you, my Lord, well skill'd to cater,

Resolv'd in Mind, compos'd in Feature,

Seiz'd on the Bowels of the Traitor ;

And,

And, Vultur-like, eat piping hot

The Liver of rebellious Scot.

Tell me no more of Turtle-Eaters,

Hogs barbecu'd, and monftrous Creatures,

Devour'd by Aldermen and Prætors:

What Member of a Calves-Head Party

E'er din'd fo loyal and fo hearty?

'Tis true, fome Men of Tafte and Breeding

Copy your Lordfhip's Mode of Feeding,

And *comme il faut* their Fingers greafe

With rotten Cabbage, *Limburgh* Cheefe,

Italian Pafte, and Dainties more

Than grac'd th' *Apician* Board of Yore;

Tranfported when they meet with Difhes,

That anfwer to their ardent Wifhes;

In Raptures they'll the Cook embrace,

Saluting him, with *French* Grimace,

On both Sides of his greasy Face ;

So have they learnt, in foreign Parts,

T' adore the culinary Arts,

And soon, in Eating's noble Science,

May hope to bid the World Defiance.

A roasted Bear did no small Credit

To those who eat, and those who fed it ;

But in these dreadful Days of Famine,

While one half of the World is cramming,

And t'other rioting and damning,

K—g, Lords, and Commons, all must own,

A Nation's Thanks are your's alone ;

Your Men of Art, and Science too,

Their Premium shall assign to you,

E   To

To you the Palm, who firſt ſuch Food
Invented for the public Good,
And ſhew'd at once to all Mankind
Your Country's Love, your Taſte refin'd.
* Thus, when from Heav'n the Pow'rs divine
Came down with TANTALUS to dine,
The *Lydian* King, his Banquet to improve,
On human Fleſh regal'd, and taught great JOVE
To add one Dainty to his Feaſts above.

Sweet Patron of the Muſe's Lyre,
PHOEBUS, if e'er thou didſt inſpire
One modern Bard with *Theban* Fire,

* Pind. Olymp. 1. lin. 56

Taught

Taught Him aloft, from Garret Win*der*,

To found the deep-ton'd Shell of PINDAR,

And catch his heav'nly Flame like Tinder,

    Fly through the liquid Air,

    Be BROUGHTON's Games thy Care,

And all thy golden Shafts be there.

Bid CLIO quit her blest Abode,

And speed her Flight to *Oxford-Road*,

Adore the Theatre of BROUGHTON,

And kiss the Stage his Lordship fought on ;

Let all his Battles be recounted,

By-Battles, till the Masters mounted,

Ere yet the tender Down began

To shade his Chin, and promise Man :

Tell, to what Deeds of bold Emprize

We saw his manly Strength arise ;

                                  Superior

Superior to the mean Events

Of little warlike Accidents,

Which ftill might greatly difcompofe

The Features of our modern Beaux,

And from their *Macaroni* Faces

Send packing all the Loves and Graces;

Two batter'd Jaws, a flatten'd Snout,

Depending like a broken Spout,

And Wifdom at one Eye fhut out.

Nathlefs the Hero, undifinay'd,

Purfues the bold *Olympic* Trade,

Snuffs up a Battle from afar,

And trains the hardy Youth to War;

Ne'er mourns one Minifter of Light,

Condemn'd in ever-during Night

To roll and find no Dawn, while t'other

Does double Duty for it's Brother;

And when two Chiefs of like Renown

Grappling conteſt the *Pythian* Crown,

The Gods, delighted, oft' ſurvey

His ſingle Orb, with piercing Ray,

Twinkling direct the doubtful Fray.

Such, though from Heaven it ſo far be,

Well-pleas'd, of late they view'd at *Derby*,

When Diſcord rag'd, and Wrath grew higher,

Betwixt the NAILOR and the DYER:

Stern was the Fight; one PALLAS fir'd,

And t'other MARS himſelf inſpir'd,

* 'Till JOVE, who knew their ſtubborn Spirits,

Call'd for his Scales, to weigh their Merits;

* Καὶ τότε δὴ χρύσεια πατὴρ ἐτίταινε τάλαντα, &c. Hom. Il. 22. lin. 209.

F   And

And all the Deities allow,

Such Sport was ne'er beheld till now.

O! may fome Bard refound the Theme,

From *Derwent*'s Banks to *Thames*'s Stream.!.

Immortalize fuch **Deeds divine** ·

In far fublimer Strains than mine !.

Nor let their Praifes be omitted,

Who two fuch gallant Heroes pitted,

Forfook their Cards, Dice, Cocks, and Stud;,

For deeper Bets on human Blood :

Yet not the DYER, or the NAILOR,.

Can equal half his paffive Valour ;.

No Bruifer, fam'd in ancient Story,

Tranfcend his perfevering Glory.

E'en the ftern Mafter of the fev'n-fold Shield,.

Who forc'd the doughty *Trojan* from the Field ;

E'en

E'en the Dictator, who by yielding won

His tardy Triumphs o'er *Amilcar*'s Son,

The *Libyan* Chiefs from fair *Tarentum* drove,

And bore their Spoils to Capitolian JOVE,

Submit to BUCKHORSE in the fame Degree

As Water yields to Gin, or *Scotch* Baubee

To CÆSAR's golden Face.—Permit, my Lord,

  The Mufe who tunes her Throat

  To Victory's gladfome Note,

The black-ey'd Nymph THALIA to record

What erft thefe Eyes beheld.——

  'Twas at the *Weftminfter* Election,

  When factious Chiefs brew'd Infurrection,

  A boift'rous independant Wight,

  Confiding in his giant Might,

  Provok'd thee to th' athletic Fight;

Arraign'd

Arraign'd thy free, thy Britifh Spirit,

And fet at nought thy patriot Merit ;

With Look malign, and Taunt fevere,

Swore that your Lordfhip's Fate was near,

And whifper'd *Tyburn* in thine Ear.

I heard the Wretch thy Mother curfe,

With Language vile, Invective worfe

Than reigns at *Billingfgate*, or even

At the fam'd Chapel of St. ST—PH—N ;

While you ferene, with confcious Virtue,

Pull'd off your Waiftcoat, and your Shirt too,

And many a Bang, and many a Cuff,

Undauntedly fuftain'd in Buff.

But what I deem your Lordfhip's Fort, is,

You lay collected like a Tortoife,

Suffer'd

Suffer'd the Caitiff to beſtride

And bruiſe thine unrelenting Hide,

'Till, prodigal of Strength, the Foe

Such Toil no more could undergo,

And, quite exhauſted, ſat him down,

Thinking the Laurels all his own :

But you, who found you'd got no Harm yet,

Firſt peep'd from underneath your Armpit,

Then, to the Joy of all Beholders,

Rais'd up your Head above your Shoulders,

Pull'd up your Breeches, ſcratch'd your Head,

Spit in your Hands, and roll'd your Quid ;

And then, like ſome great Rhetorician,

Of *Greek* and *Roman* Erudition,

In Senates us'd to wield with Eaſe

The Thunder of Demosthenes,

G   Open'd

Open'd your Budget to harangue him,

Before you undertook to bang him,

Thinking the Hero well might bear

One fhort Philippic in his Ear.

" Doft thou traduce the BUCKHORSE Name,

" And taint my virtuous Mother's Fame ;

" Blood of a Bitch! doft thou prefume

" At *Tyburn* to announce my Doom ?

" Think'ft thou, by Devils hatch'd, to quell

" My patriotic Principle ?

" Hell blaft thine Eyes, thou Mifcreant bafe,

" And Pillory feize thy ruthlefs Face,

" Ugly as *Newgate* Steps. ——

" Witnefs ye pure, ye virtuous Tribes,

" Unmov'd by Penfions and by Bribes, ·

" If

" If e'er I pouch'd one fingle Farthing,

" Since *by G-d's Grace* I've known the Garden ;

" E'er taken one unbritifh Meafure,

" To ftain my Hands with public Treafure :

" Say, have I tamper'd with the Stocks?

" (Behold this Brafs Tobacco Box,

" Fair Freedom's Boon) have I play'd booty ?——

" At *Tott'nham-Court* I've done my Duty.——

" Afk of yon Stage, where late I fought,

" Afk BROUGHTON's felf, if e'er I fought

" One dirty Job—ambition'd aught

" But GILES's Welfare!——

" Yet ftill if Gentlemen concur

" My Poft of Honour to transfer,

" In abler Hands my Office fix ;

" ---I'm ready to refign my Sticks.

" Still

" Still ſhall I live to wipe my Breech

" With thy laſt Words and dying Speech ;

" And your damn'd Figure, in a Halter,

" Shall ſmoak on CLOACINA's Altar ;

" But now, thou Spawn of Whoredom, now is

" The Time to ſhew thy Strength and Prowefs ;

" Gird well thy Loins, for I this Day

" With Intereſt thy Blows will pay."

You ſpoke---and put a Look ſedate on,

Bold as when MICHAEL frown'd on SATAN,

Then, with the rapid Lightning's Speed,

Drove, like a batt'ring Ram, thine Head,

Plump in his Paunch ; the Chief aſtounded,

Back like a Culverin rebounded.

* As

* As when some Man of Taste thinks proper

To cover o'er his House with Copper,

If chance descends nocturnal Jove

In Storms of Hailstones from above,

The Garreteer, with wild Affright,

Starts from the balmy Blessings of the Night,

Through all the live-long Hours condemn'd to hear

The echoing Dome re-bellow to his Ear ;

Thus was the valiant Wight confounded,

His clatt'ring Cheeks and Temples founded ;

While you with frequent Fist assail'd him,

With Chuckers in the Mazzard nail'd him,

And Clicks upon the Muns regal'd him ;

* ———— ———— *Quam multâ Grandine Nimbi*
Culminibus crepitant, &..

Virg. Æneid 5. lin. 45°.

Nor didſt thou not amuſe with Leggers,

Croſs-Buttocks, flying Mares, and Peggers,

Fall with your Elbows in the Bellows,

Scatter the Grinders, cloſe the Smellers,

Darken the Day-Lights!—Muſe, be brief——

You ſaw the Store-Room of the Chief

Surrender it's Election Beef,

Reluctant Dumpling, Beer, and Gravy,

And heard each groaning Bowel cry—*Peccavi.*

Think not, my Lord, I join the Crew

Who Flatt'ry's menial Arts purſue,

Unenvy'd let the ſervile Throng

Their Patrons lull with venal Song,

Ne'er was I vers'd in Dedication,

Or trod the Paths of Adulation:

May

May I be doom'd all Day to wait

The Iffue of fome dull Debate,

In *Robin Hood*'s well-crouded Senate;

(Which, Thanks to Heav'n, but once I've been at,

And then the *Baker's Man* made free

To take me into Cuftody.)

But, what is worfe, may you refufe

The Labours of my faithful Mufe,

If aught in Flattery I mention,

In Hopes of Bifhoprick or Penfion;

I know your Modefty is fuch,

You hate to be admir'd too much;

But if your Lordfhip had commanded,

The Troops that Day Prince *Ferdinand* did,

On *Minden*'s Plains the *Gallic* Foe

Had met their final Overthrow;

To you the Senate had decreed

A Statue, for thy glorious Meed,

Returning, like *Germanic* CÆSAR,

Triumphant from the Banks of *Wezer*.

Perhaps your Lordſhip may declare,

You hate a continental War,

That you from Childhood was afraid

Of Powder, Balls, and Cannonade;

Why didſt thou then, with Patriot Zeal,

Illume the Rocket-loaded Wheel,

Big with Combuſtion, when ſuch Praiſe

Redounded from the Peace of *Aix ?*

And this triumphant frugal Nation,

To liſt'ning *Europe*'s Admiration,

Made all her Cannon echo louder

Than thund'ring JOVE ; and ſpent her Powder,

As

As freely as our warlike Swains

Affembled on their peaceful Plains,

To fcorch their Fingers, Wigs, and Nofes,

Firing—*pro Aris et pro Focis.*

Say why, my Lord?——but lo! the Mufe

No more thefe arduous Themes purfues;

Unable thy Exploits to fing,

Trembling fhe checks her tow'ring Wing,

Speeds to domeftic Scenes of Life,

Sighs to falute thy virtuous Wife.

O! may ye long unparted prove

The Bleffings of connubial Love,

Live to exhibit, in this queer Age,

A bright Example to the Peerage;

Grace *Marybone,* your ancient Seat,

And *Hockley-Hole's* fecure Retreat,

I

Where

Where you, as quiet and serene as

Great *Africanus,* or *Mæcenas,*

From Toils of State, from Noise and Care,

To calm Retirement's Joys repair:

While Lady Buckhorse tunes her Throat

To many a soft love-labour'd Note,

Culls each *Burletta* Strain she heard in

The comic Op'ras of the Garden,

And teaches Trivia to repeat

Italian Airs, in *English* Ditties sweet.

Much would your Lordship's Erudition

Improve such sprightly Composition ;

And should some Bard, in future Years,

Collect the Works of modern Peers,

(If right I augur) 'twill be thine

First in the noble List to shine.

O !

O ! may your Candour, Tafte, and Eafe,

Inftruct my artlefs Mufe to pleafe;

* May ev'ry bolder Stroke be heighten'd,

And by your abler Pencil brighten'd ;

So fhall I raife my future Song

High above all the tuneful Throng,

Boafting, as once the comic Bard did,

That *Lælius* all my Toils rewarded :

So may the Gods attend my Pray'r,

And make thy hopeful Son and Heir,

Young BUCKHORSE, their peculiar Care;

Whofe Virtues, like fair Flow'rs, expand,

Rais'd by your Lordfhip's foft'ring Hand ;

Tranfplanted from *Newmarket* Races

To *Alma Mater*'s chafte Embraces,

* Vide Middleton.

Where

Where late he came, with Refolution

T' obferve each pious Inftitution,

With filial Duty to regard her;

(Example rare!) and with fuch Ardour

Purfu'd his academic Studies,

As worthy of his noble Blood is:

Here did he woo the modeft Nine,

And tune their Inftruments divine;

So much improve his nat'ral Parts,

That in three Weeks he won our Hearts,

And gain'd a Mafterfhip of Arts.

Now travels far the *Alps* beyond,

Of more polite Amufements fond,

In which, I hope, and muft fuppofe fo,

He'll foon become a Virtuofo.

Kind

Kind Heav'n protect him! Safe from Harms

Reftore him to his Country's Arms,

In *Britain*'s public Pofts to join

The Heroes of the Patriot Line :

Then may we hope once more to fee

The fmiling Days of Liberty,

When Son and Sire at once efpoufes

Her facred Caufe in both their Houfes,

And each his Influence extends

To Virtue only and her Friends :

Pleas'd that fuch patriotic Souls

Will condefcend to drain his Bowls,

WILDMAN once more his Houfe refuming,

In Tranfports fhall his Lights relumine.—

And when (may Heav'n ordain it late)

Your Lordfhip fhall fubmit to Fate,

K

When

When, after many a well-fought Field,

Yourfelf to conq'ring Death fhall yield,

(As yield you muft, and that bright Eye

Add Glory to it's kindred Sky)

You fhall for ever be THE NOTED,

And I to diftant Ages quoted,

  My Lord,

    Your Lordfhip's:

      moft devoted;.

Cambridge,
Dec. 1, 1767.

      P O S T S C R I P T.

My Lord, it grieves me to relate

The worthy Dr. BOLTER's Fate ;

            He

He found his Appetite decreas'd

E'er since the Visitation Feast,

Sent for Advice, but sent in vain,

For all the *Æsculapian* Train

Were met that Week in *Warwick-Lane*;

Where certain peaceful learned Leeches,

With Hammers, Iron-Crows, and Speeches,

And Blacksmiths arm'd, were making Entries

By Ways unknown to *Coke* and *Ventris*,

While other harmless Sons of GALEN,

These barb'rous civil Feuds bewailing,

Prepar'd their Engines for assailing:

So while, his Dignity asserting,

Old Dr. SQUILLS behind the Curtain,

Pointed his Leathern Tube to play on

His Friend Sir OXYMEL MAC'HAON,

Seiz'd

Seiz'd with an Hiccup, Flux, and Phthific,

—Th' Archdeacon dy'd, for Want of Phyfic ;—

By which your *Toadland* Living's vacant,

—I beg your Lordfhip not to fpeak on't ;—

(For previous to a Man's Interment,

G-d knows I feek not his Preferment :)

But, as I've taken my Degree,

And grow impatient to be free,

—I wifh, my Lord, you'd think on me.

And if, my Lord, your Lordfhip chufes

A Man of *all Work* for your Mufes,

(Such as, for great Men's private Ufes,

This Seat of Learning oft' produces)

To clean a Buskin, or a Sandal,—

To hear you fpout, and hold the Candle,—

To fire your Crackers in the Papers,—

To cure unpenfion'd Friends of Vapours,—

Do dirty Jobs about the Houfe too,—

I am the Man that you may truft to;

And humbly beg, that you'll incline

To make that pleafing Office mine.——

Indulge me ftill one more Requeft, Sir,

T' oblige my worthy Friend Sylvester;

Who, from your Lordfhip's Grace and Bounty,

Hopes to be Sheriff for the County;

Fir'd with a gen'rous Emulation

T' excel in that important Station,

His Beeves, his Sheep, the 'Squire devotes

To Lace, to Liveries, Hats and Coats;

L   And

And gives us to expect next Year all
A grand Affembly in the Shire-Hall:
E'en now his venerable Coach is
New gilding, ere th' Affize approaches ;
No longer at the Tax repining,
Tranfported he reviews the Lining,
Which he remembers, when a Boy,
Was fafhionable brown Cafoy;
Now like your Lordfhip's Face appears
Well-worn, but not fubdu'd by Years :
Oft' dreams he of Election Journies,
Writs, Jailors, Hangmen, and Attornies,
Of Trumpets echoing in his Ears,
 Full-bottom'd Periwigs, and Spears ;
Hears Voices at a Diftance humming,
" *Make Way, make Way---The* SHRIEVE's *a coming.*"

Then

Then in his balmy Sleep he trudges

With milk-white Wand, before the Judges;

Or thinks, in Velvet Coat array'd, he

Meets at the Ball his frizzled Lady,

Who looks half pleas'd, and half affrighted,

E'er fince her Husband has been knighted. ——

Yet ftill, my Lord, with due Submiffion,

Before you realize his Vifion,

The 'Squire entreats you'd *   *   *   *

* * * * * * * * * * * *

* * * * * * * * * * * *

* * * * *Defunt multa.* * * *

* * * * * * * * * * * *

* * * * * * * * * * *

Then

Then, to requite your Lordſhip's Favour,

I hope he'll uſe his beſt Endeavour,   -

As one good Turn demands another,

To make RETURNS to ſerve your Brother.

F I N I S.

www.ingramcontent.com/pod-product-compliance
Lightning Source LLC
Chambersburg PA
CBHW030910260626
47169CB00008B/2780